Lovingly Presented

To _____

From _____

On _____

*Jesus loves
the little children*

Dedicated with love to my grandchildren
Ashley, Lauren and Kevin Shannon
and
To all children everywhere.

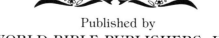

Published by
WORLD BIBLE PUBLISHERS, INC.
Iowa Falls, Iowa

CHRISTIAN MOTHER GOOSE®

Rock-A-Bye Prayers

A Blessing Book

Selected Scripture from
The Authorized King James Version

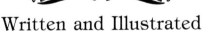

Written and Illustrated
by
Marjorie Ainsborough Decker

A PRAYER FROM
CHRISTIAN MOTHER GOOSE

Bless the little children,
　Dear Father God;
They are very little.
　Thank You for
　Your bigness
In which their little ways
　May walk and talk
In safety, ever growing
　In the knowledge
　And grace of
Our Lord Jesus Christ;
　The love of God;
And the fellowship of
　The Holy Spirit.

Amen.

May this collection of little prayers,
especially written for you and your little
loved ones, truly be a Blessing Book of
little windows into the loving, big heart
of our Father God.

With love,
Marjorie Ainsborough Decker

A LOT OF LOVE

Dear God, it takes a lot of rain
To wash the world's big face.
Dear God, it takes a lot of love
To show the world Your grace.
A big, big world with lots of need,
A big, big world for You to feed.
Dear God, it takes a lot of love
To show the world Your grace.

*God . . . for His great love
wherewith He loved us.*
Eph. 2:4

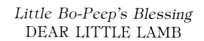

Little Bo-Peep's Blessing
DEAR LITTLE LAMB

Dear little lamb,
Do you know,
That Jesus Christ
Was called a lamb
Long, long ago?

Dear little lamb,
Do you know,
That Jesus came
To save us
For He loves us so?

Dear little lamb,
With soft, white fleece,
Do you know
That Jesus
Is the Prince of Peace?

Dear little lamb,
What happy story!
Do you know
The Lamb of God
Is King of glory!

6

The lamb . . . he is Lord of Lords,
and king of kings. Rev. 17:14

Dear little lamb,
Both you and I,
  Shall bow before
  His lovely throne
  By and by.

LEARNING TO COUNT

Dear Lord, I learned
To count today,
And this is what
I'd like to say:
"Thanks for fingers,
One through ten,
For that's the way
I learned! Amen."

RUB-A-DUB-DUB PRAYER

Rub-a-dub-dub,
Three prayers from a tub,
With bubbles and prayers
Side by side.
"Dear God, as we scrub
On the *out*side, and rub,
Please rub-a-dub
Scrub us *in*side."

Create in me a clean heart,
O God. Psalm 51:10

9

FARTHING SPARROW'S PRAYER

Thank You, Lord,
For little people,
Bringing food
For us each day.
Sometimes seeds,
And sometimes bread;
Please bless them,
Good and kind are they.

Thank You, Lord,
For bigger people,
Building homes
With roof and eaves,
Where a sparrow
There can nestle,
When the trees
Have lost their leaves.

11

MEMORIES

Dear Lord, for all
The happy times
With Mom and Dad, today,
I thank You
For the memories
That I can tuck away.

I thank my God upon every remembrance of you. Phil. 1:3

A LITTLE PRAYER

Dear God, this is a little prayer,
For I am little, too:
"I love You because
You first loved me;
Thank You,"
Now I'm through.

*We love Him, because He
first loved us. I John 4:19*

Little Nancy Etticoat's
LITTLE PRAYER

This little prayer
  Is for Mother.
This little prayer
  Is for Dad.
This little prayer
  Is for children,
To keep them safe and glad.
  And this little prayer
  Is to share with those
  Who have no one to pray. . .

Humpty Dumpty's Prayer
IT'S RAINING, IT'S POURING

It's raining, it's pouring,
God's blessings on the town;
For all the little children
Are praying blessings down!

*God... who shall bless thee
with blessings of heaven
above. Gen. 49:25*

ESPECIALLY LOVED

For little children
  Who cannot see,
I pray they will
  Especially be
Especially loved,
Especially dear,
To all who know them
  Far and near;
And that in Jesus'
  Arms they'll rest,
For He's the One
  Who loves them best.

A Prayer From Tommy Tucker
LITTLE RABBIT

Little rabbit in the snow,
    Lying still,
    Do you know
A little boy came by today,
    He stroked your fur,
    Then knelt to pray:
"Dear Lord Who watches over all,
Protect these little creatures small."

*I will pray for you unto
the Lord.* I Sam. 7:5

Well done, good and faithful servant. Mat. 25:23

WELL DONE!

Dearest Jesus,
God's dear Son,
Here my journey's just begun;
As a child I'll follow You,
Step by step in all I do.
Dearest Jesus,
Savior, Friend,
When I reach my journey's end,
Bringing children I have won,
May I hear Your words:
"WELL DONE!"

MARY'S PSALM

The Lord is my Shepherd
So kind and so good;
I love Him and follow Him,
As all children should.
The Lord is my Shepherd,
He knows the safe way;
He loves me and leads me
To His house to stay.

The Lord is my Shepherd;
I shall not want.
Psalm 23:1

A PRAYER TO SPARE

Dear Father up in Heaven,
I have a prayer to spare;
Please take it for
A lonely child
Who needs it now, somewhere.

TOMMY TITTLEMOUSE'S PRAYER

Dear God, I'm just a tittle-mouse,
Not needing much at all;
Thank You for the wayside crumbs,
And tasty seeds that fall.

Who giveth food to all flesh:
for His mercy endureth for ever.
Psa. 136:25

MORNING MERCIES

Holy Father,
Holy Son,
Holy Spirit,
Day is done.
Darkness cannot
Hide Your face,
I am safe
In Your embrace.

The Lord's mercies . . . are new every morning. Lam. 3:22,23

Holy Father,
Holy Son,
Holy Spirit,
Day has come!
Fresh with morning
Mercies new,
I offer up
My thanks to You.

Lucy Locket's Prayer
TO SHOW MY LOVE

Dear God, I'd like to tell You. . .
To show my love for Mommy,
I helped her make my bed.
To show my love for Daddy,
I did the things he said.
To show my love for Grandma,
I sent a little letter;
To show my love for Grandpa,
I prayed he would get better.
To show my love for You,
And dear Jesus up above,
I did those things
You said to do,
Because You gave me love.

*When thou liest down,
thou shalt not be afraid.*
Provers 3:24

AT BEDTIME

Dear God in Heaven, I bow my head,
Here beside my little bed;
In Your loving care, I'm blest,
While I sleep, safe at rest.

LITTLE MISSIONARY

Dear Lord, I saw some pictures
All of children far away.
They looked so sad and lonely,
That I promised I would pray.
I feel so sad and sorry
As I pray for them tonight,
Because these little children
Haven't learned to read or write.
I'll share my piggy-bank, Lord,
So that I can help to send
A missionary teacher
Who will help them, as Your friend.

A Diller, A Dollar's Prayer
OFF TO SCHOOL

Dear God, as off to school I go,
My heart is happy, for I know
That You are with me, always there,
To keep me in Your loving care.

The Lord thy God is with thee,
whithersoever thou goest.
Joshua 1:9

Little Polly Flinders' Prayer
THE NARROW PATH

I saw a little path
In the meadow, soft and sweet;
Only big enough
For my two little feet.
So narrow was the path,
That I couldn't go astray;
It led me straight to our house
As I followed all the way.

I am the way, the truth, and the life. John 14:6

Then I remembered, Jesus,
You said You are the Way
To God the Father's house,
So I'm kneeling here to pray:

*"Dear Jesus, put my feet
On Your straight and narrow way;
And lead me up to Heaven,
To the Father's house, someday."*

Little Jumping Joan's Prayer
THANK YOU, GOD, FOR EVERYTHING

Thank You, God, for rain and sun;
Eyes to see with, legs to run.
Friends to play with; birds to sing;
Thank You, God, for everything!

Jack and Jill's Prayer
BOYS AND GIRLS
COME OUT TO PRAY

Boys and girls
Come out to pray.
The Lord has brought
A brand new day,
Filled with many
Wondrous things,
To make us glad,
To make us sing!
Come and join us
As we pray:
"Thank You God,
For this new day!"

*In the morning will I direct my
prayer unto thee.* Psalm 5:3

THANK YOU FOR THE BIBLE

Thank You for the Bible, Lord,
The Book the Spirit penned;
Telling us of Your great love,
From beginning to the end.
Thank You for the Bible, Lord,
That taught me to believe
On Jesus Christ, The Son of God,
My Savior to receive.

— Amen

A Prayer From Little Boy Blue
DEAR BABY JESUS

Dear Baby Jesus,
  You seemed, oh, so small,
To bring down to earth
  God's great love for us all.
Yet such a small seed
  As an acorn, I know,
Is what God has given
  For oak trees to grow.
So, dear Baby Jesus,
  God's own precious Seed,
You filled all the world
  With God's love and good deeds.

*For unto you is born this day . . .
a Saviour, which is Christ the Lord.*
Luke 2:11

JUST LIKE THEE

Dear Lord Jesus, make me to be
Kind and loving, just like thee.
Quick to help, quick to love,
Quick to pray to the Father above.
Dear Lord Jesus, make me to be
Kind and loving, just like Thee.

*Be ye followers of God,
as dear children.* Eph. 5:1

GRANDPA DANDELIONS

Dear God, You made
  Young dandelions
Bright and yellow gold.
  Sprinkled them
  Around me
For me to pick and hold.
  Then later on
  The dandelions
All turn from gold to gray;
  But they're the ones
  Who rise up in the air
To fly away!
  They make me think
  Of my Grandpa,
When he had turned gray, too,
  Like Grandpa dandelions
He flew away to be with You!

Come before His presence
with thanksgiving.
Psalm 95:2

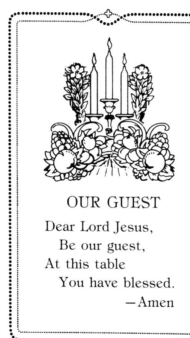

OUR GUEST

Dear Lord Jesus,
Be our guest,
At this table
You have blessed.
—Amen

Miss Muffet's Prayer
JESUS TAUGHT US

Jesus taught us we should pray,
Thanking God for food each day;
So with thankful hearts we raise
Prayers of thanks,
And prayers of praise.

He took bread and blessed it. Luke 24:30

JOHN

Today I was a chimney-sweep,
With a brush and tall black hat;
And then I was a puppy
Hiding underneath the mat.
When everyone had found me,
I turned into a bear!
"Have you seen John,"
They asked me,
"We're sure he's here somewhere."
I growled and growled so loud
That they ran away in fright;
So I stayed a hungry bear
All through supper-time, tonight.

But, now I'm tucked in bed, Lord,
And the others cannot see,
I'm not a chimney-sweep or bear,
I'm John, and he is me!
Dear God, it's John who's praying,
Please be with me in the dark,
And when the daylight comes again,
I think I'll be a shark!

Suffer the little children to come unto me. Mark 10:14

Simple Simon's Prayer
LEARNING TO PRAY

Dear Lord,
I thought there had to be
A special kind of way
To bow my head,
And close my eyes,
To learn how I should pray.
But then I learned of Jesus,
And it's simple as can be;
To pray is just
To talk to Him
Who said, "Come unto Me."

MISTRESS MARY'S
GARDEN PRAYER

Dear God in Heaven, I thank You
For every tree and flower.
For meadows green to play in;
For sunshine and each hour.
For gardens we can grow;
For raindrops as they fall;
For family, home and friends;
I thank You for them all.

Let my mouth be filled with
thy praise and thy honour . . .
Psa. 71:8

41

IF I ONLY KNEW

If I only knew
Three little words,
I would want them to be
The very best words
In all the world;
Those words are:
"God loves me!"

If I only knew
One lovely name,
I would want it to be
The very best name
In all the world;
That Name is
"Jesus" to me!

GOD IS LOVE

God is love,
God is light,
God is all
That's good
And right.

God is love. I John 4:16

HAPPY PRAYERS

Happy thoughts
Make happy prayers,
And happy faces say,
"How nice it is
When God can see me
Smiling when I pray.

Whoso trusteth in the Lord,
happy is he. Prov. 16:20

ROBIN REDBREAST'S PRAYER

There are two little eggs, Lord,
Tucked in my cozy nest.
Please keep them warm
And safe from harm,
That they may sing their best.
And should some curious children
On tip-toe take a look,
Remind them not to touch them,
As You said in Your good Book.

Jack-Be-Nimble's Prayer
FRIENDS

Thank you, Lord, for friends,
Friends you send and lend,
Friends to love and play with,
Whether short or tall.
Stormy-weather friends;
All-together friends;
Furry-feather friends;
Dear Lord, You gave them all.

*There is a friend that sticketh
closer than a brother.*
Prov. 18:24

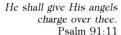

Bobby Shaftoe's Prayer
GUARDIAN ANGELS

Dear God, Who sends the angels
   To guard each girl and boy,
Please send an angel
   Who can share with me
Some fishing joy.

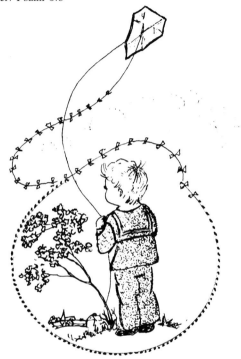

FLY, LITTLE PRAYER

Little prayer, go fly, fly, fly!
Past the stars up in the sky.
Little prayer — my very own,
Reach my Heavenly Father's throne.

MY HEART

Dear God,
  My heart is open wide,
For Jesus, Lord,
  To come inside;
There, forever, to abide,
  My Savior and my Friend.

*As many as received Him,
to them gave He power to
become the sons of God.*
John 1:12

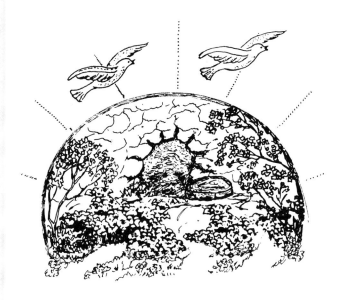

EASTER TIME!

Easter time, Easter time!
Everything is singing.
Easter time, Easter time!
Easter voices ringing.
Easter sunshine fills the sky;
Easter birds sing as they fly;
Angel choirs sing on high;
"THE LORD IS RISEN!"

Easter time, Easter time!
Easter flowers in bloom;
Easter time, Easter time!
Easter's empty tomb!
Boys and girls are bringing
Easter hearts a-singing:
"CHRIST IS RISEN,
PRAISE THE LORD!"
It's Easter time!

*Jesus of Nazareth, which was
crucified, He is risen.*
Mark 16:6

FORGIVENESS

Dear God, the sun is going down,
So before its light is gone,
I ask You to forgive me
For the wrongs I may have done.
And I forgive each one and all
Who may have wronged me, too.
Thank You for forgiveness;
Now I'll sleep
The whole night through.

ROUND AND ROUND THE TABLE

Round and round the table,
We join our hands in prayer:
  "Thank You, Lord,
  For food and drink,
  And fellowship we share."
Round and round the table,
We join our hands in prayer:
  "Thank You, Lord,
  For each of us,
  And for Your tender care."
                    Amen.

*Thou preparest a table
before me.* Psalm 23:5

PLEASING TO THEE

Help me, dear Lord
  My thoughts to be,
Lovely and good;
  Pleasing to Thee.
Help me, dear Lord,
  My words to be,
Gracious and kind;
  Pleasing to Thee.
Help me, dear Lord,
  My ways to be,
Faithful and true;
  Pleasing to Thee.
                —Amen

*Do those things that
are pleasing in His
sight.* I John 3:22

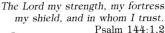

The Lord my strength, my fortress
my shield, and in whom I trust.
Psalm 144:1,2

Little Jack Horner's Prayer
ASLEEP IN MY CASTLE

Dear God, I'm in my castle,
(Though it looks like a wooden bed).
My soldiers all have gone to sleep,
So I thank You that You said,
 "The Lord will keep my castle,
 And let no one through the door."
Because You're strong, and never sleep,
My castle's safe and sure.

Grandpa Mole's
"SHUSH NOW"

Shush, now,
Shush, now,
Everybody hush, now,
All of Heaven
Is listening
To hear what children say.

Shush, now,
Shush, now ,
Everybody hush, now,
Even angels
Fold their wings
When little children pray.

Mother Hubbard's Prayer
BLESSINGS BIG, BLESSINGS SMALL

Blessings big, blessings small;
Dearest Jesus gave them all.
Children big, children small,
Come and praise Him,
One and all!

Our Lord Jesus Christ, who hath
blessed us with all spiritual
blessings. Eph. 1:3

GOD BLESS OUR LAND

God bless our land,
   That it may be
A safe and happy
   Place for me.
God bless our land,
   That it may be
A place that loves
   And trusts in Thee.

*Blessed is the nation
whose God is the Lord.*
Psalm 33:12

GOD IS HERE!

Dear God, I saw the sparkling frost
  On daisy fields today.
Each little daisy with a crown,
  So lovely, seemed to say:
    "God is here! God is here!
    That's how daisy crowns appear."

Dear God, I saw the sparkling smile
  On Mommy's face today.
Each little smile she gave to me,
  So lovely, seemed to say:
    "God is here! God is here!
    That's how loving smiles appear."

He is altogether lovely.
Song 5:16

Thank You, God, for being here,
Over there, and everywhere!
That's how lovely things appear...
"God is here! God is here!"

FILL MY HEART

Dear Lord Jesus, strong and true,
Fill my heart with love for You.
Love for Father, love for Mother,
Love for sister, love for brother,
Love for friend, and family too,
Love to tell the world of You!

—Amen

GENTLE JESUS

Gentle Jesus, meek and mild,
Loving every little child,
　　Teach us all
　　That we may be
Gentle boys and girls like Thee.

The fruit of the Spirit is
. . . gentleness. Gal. 5:22

JESUS CARES

Jesus cares when I am sick,
  So I tell Him
  Quick, quick, quick!
  "Thank You!
  In the Bible's letter
You made little children better."

*Jesus . . . went about healing
all manner of sickness.*
Mat. 4:23

Out of the mouths of babes
thou hast perfected praise.
Mat. 21:16

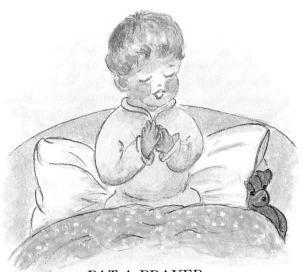

PAT-A-PRAYER

Pat-A-Prayer,
Pat-A-Prayer,
Little one.
Clap your hands,
Say a prayer
To God's dear Son:
"Bless the little children,
Jesus, day and night;
They are of Your kingdom,
And precious in Your sight."

65

COVERING UP

Dear God, I made a stain today
On Mommy's cloth,
And I ran away.
Then I crept back,
And covered it up
With pretty flowers
In a pretty cup.
Then I remembered, "God will know;
He sees the stain
That doesn't show!"
So I told Mommy,
(She didn't shout),
She smiled, and said,
"I'll wash it out!

*Wash me, and I shall be whiter
than snow.* Psalm 51:7

But here's a lesson we should know:
    God washes *our* stains
    White as snow,
    When we don't hide,
    And cover them up
    With pretty flowers
    In a pretty cup."
*"So, Good Night, God, I'm glad to know,
Just as I am, You love me so!"*

He giveth His beloved sleep.
Psalm 127:2

NOD, NOD, NOD

Sometimes, when I pray to God,
My little head goes
Nod, Nod, Nod.
That's because it's time for bed,
And I've become a sleepy-head.
But I'd much rather fall asleep
Saying prayers, than counting sheep!

The Lord bless thee, and keep thee.
Num. 6:24

HERE IS THE CHURCH

Here is the church,
Here is the steeple;
Here are the prayers
Of God's little people:

"Thank You, Lord Jesus,
Our Savior so true;
You'll take us to Heaven
Because we love You."

The Jolly Miller's Prayer
HANDS

The farmer's hands,
The ploughman's hands,
The harvester's as well;
The miller's hands,
The baker's hands,
The hands of those who sell;
The father's hands,
The mother's hands,
All join to bring us food;
So we thank God
For all of them,
With prayers of gratitude.

But all the hands
Of everyone,
Would empty be, indeed,
Without the hands
Of our good God,
Who gave the soil and seed!

*God may bless thee in all the work
of thine hands.* Deut. 24:19

THERE IS NO OTHER
GOD BUT YOU!

Dear God, I am so proud of You;
There is no other God but You!
      Making pumpkins,
      Making trees,
      Making berries,
      Making bees,
      Making rainbows,
      Making snow,
      Making 'now',
      And 'long ago',

I am the Lord, and there is none else. Isaiah 45:6

Making mountains,
Making sea,
Making land,
Making me!
Making all
The stars above,
Making us
To know Your love.
Dear God, I am so proud of You,
There is no other God but You!

ME

Thank You, Lord,
That I can be
Just the little child
Called, "Me".
Not the same as
Bill or Sue;
But a special "Me",
With love from You.

*I will praise thee; for I am
fearfully and wonderfully
made.* Psalm 139:14

74

PRAYING TOGETHER

Daddy said a prayer;
Then I jumped into bed.
Mommy said a prayer;
Then here's the prayer I said:
"Dear God, although it's dark,
With cold, frosty weather,
I feel safe and warm
When we all pray together."
                    Amen.

Betty Botter's Prayer
THINK ON THESE THINGS

Dear God, you said to think of
What is good and what is true;
What is pure and lovely,
I should think them
Through and through.
But as I go to sleep tonight,
With thoughts so good and true,
Dear Jesus, I just want to say,
These thoughts are all of YOU!

Whatsoever things are true . . .
pure . . . lovely, think on
these things. Phil. 4:8

The father to the children shall
make known thy truth.
Isa. 38:19

THANK YOU FOR DADDY

Dear Lord, I want to thank You
  For the time that Daddy took,
To read to me tonight
  From my favorite picture book.
Thank You for my Daddy,
  I love him, yes I do;
And he loves me, and I am glad
  We both love You!

IF

If little children everywhere
Would each one say a little prayer,
Then this big world would better be,
Because of children, just like me.

GOOSEY, GOOSEY, GANDER

Goosey, Goosey, Gander,
Are long prayers any grander
Than simple, little prayers
From a little girl like me?
Friend of Goosey Gander,
It is my "understander"
That, long or short,
The grandest prayers
Come from the heart, you see.

*Man looketh on the outward appearance,
but the Lord looketh on the heart.*
I Samuel 16:7

A BLESSING

God bless all those who love us;
God bless all those who care;
God bless all those who pray
For little children, everywhere.
—Amen

In blessing I will bless thee.
Gen. 22:17

SURPRISE!

Dear Father God, I hold my breath
   In wonderful surprise!
When I read You ride upon the wings
   Of wind across the skies.
Whoever thought my Father,
   With so much to do on high,
Likes to leave His throne to fly
   The wings of winds across the sky!

THANKSGIVING DAY PRAYER

Heavenly Father, here we pray,
On this great Thanksgiving Day;
Round the table, one by one,
We give thanks for all You've done.

All the blessings You provide,
Bountiful, both far and wide.
Great is all Thy faithfulness;
Great our thanks as Thee we bless.
In Jesus Name. Amen.

*Blessed be the Lord who daily
loadeth us with benefits.*
Psa. 68:19

GRANDMA'S AND GRANDPA'S

Thank You, God, for Grandma's,
And Grandpa's, too, as well.
They're specially for children,
And what stories they can tell!

Grandma's and Grandpa's
Know how to hug you tight;
They don't mind if you jump in bed
And sleep with them all night!

Grandma's and Grandpa's,
God gave to me and you.
And if you do not have one,
You should borrow one or two!

*With the ancient is wisdom; and
in length of days understanding.*
Job 12:12

A PRAYER FOR CHILDREN

For little children everywhere,
Who do not have someone to care,
Dear Lord, I pray that You will send
Each one a kind and loving friend.
                              —Amen

THE OLD SHOE-HOUSE PRAYER

Dear God in Heaven, I send my prayer
From down in the old Shoe-House;
Full of children — good little souls,
And more than one kind mouse.
I pray You'll keep our tongues in place,
Laced up with love from Mother;
Thankful for Your love and grace
To sister and to brother.
May our shoe shine with loving care,
In all we say and do.
We thank You, Lord, that we can share
The gift of love from You.

*But as for me and my house,
we will serve the Lord.*
Josh. 24:15

WHAT A HAPPY MYSTERY!

What a happy mystery!
That everything I touch and see
Began inside the earth to be
A gift so good from God to me!
What a happy mystery!
That God's Dear Son
Should live in me!
That everyone I touch and see
May know God's greatest Gift
Through me!

I WANT TO BE . . .

Dear God, I want to be a boy
Like Daniel, brave and true;
Like Joshua at Jericho,
When all the trumpets blew;
Like David fighting giant men,
But more than all of these,
I want to be like Jesus,
And my Heavenly Father please.

*I do always those things
that please Him.* John 8:29

COME, BLESS US

Dear Father up in Heaven,
Dear Jesus, Son of grace,
Dear gentle, Holy Spirit,
Come, bless us in this place.

—Amen

In thy presence is fulness of joy.
Psalm 16:11

NAP-TIME

Nap-time is lap-time,
I climb on Mommy's knee;
Nap-time is clap-time,
As Mommy reads to me.
Nap-time is happy-time,
We pray to God above;
Nap-time is lap-time,
In Mommy's lap of love.

A CHRISTMAS PRAYER

I will sing a Christmas prayer:
    Christ has come!
    Our Savior fair.
    Jesus is His
    Earthly Name,
    From the throne
    Of God He came.

Came to do
His Father's will,
Peace on earth,
To men — goodwill!
Came to live
On earth with men,
To bring us back
To God again.
I will sing a Christmas prayer:
Christ has come! Prepare! Prepare!

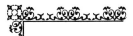

WEE WILLIE WINKIE'S PRAYER

Dear Lord, how good to see the sight
Of dear, good folk
As they say "Good Night,"

To good little children
In good little beds,
On good little pillows
For good little heads;
In good little homes,
With good little lights;
And good little prayers
To bless them each night.

Some prayers prayed in song;
Some short and some long;
A prayer that is sad;
A prayer that is glad;
A wiggling prayer;
A squiggling prayer;
From wee girl and boy,
Whose prayers You enjoy.

Behold, what manner of love the Father hath bestowed upon us . . . I John 3:1

Their prayers are the best,
North, South, East and West.
Their prayers filled with love,
To You up above.

Dear Lord, how good to see the sight
Of dear, good folk
As they say, "Good Night".

CONTENTS

CONTENTS

Marjorie Ainsborough Decker

Marjorie Decker is a #1 National Bestseller author who is well-known and loved for her distinct story-telling style.

A native of Liverpool, England, Marjorie now resides in the United States with her husband, Dale. They are parents of four grown sons.

Her Christian Mother Goose® Classics have endeared the trust of parents and the twinkle of children around the world.

Along with authoring ten books in the Christian Mother Goose® Series, Marjorie brings fresh enthusiasm and dynamic teaching to sound, Biblical scholarship. There is a pleasant nostalgia to her children's books with a curious appeal to Bible lovers of all ages . . .

Mrs. Decker is also a conference speaker to adults, a recording artist, and a frequent guest of national network television and radio.